BEWARE THE K

"A funny book, hilarious, for 6, 7 or 8-year-olds. It's about a boy who demonizes his coat! The book brings the horror round very neatly to rationally explaining what is going on in the boy's mind."
Michael Rosen, BBC Radio's Treasure Islands

Susan Gates taught English at a school in County Durham for a number of years before becoming a full-time author. She has written several books for young people, including *The Burnhope Wheel*, *Dragline*, *Deadline for Danny's Beach* and the Walker title *Beetle and the Biosphere*. She is married with three children.

Josip Lizatović designs and makes jewellery, as well as being an illustrator. *Beware the Killer Coat* is his first book.

Books by the same author

Beetle and the Biosphere

For older readers

African Dreams

The Burnhope Wheel

Deadline for Danny's Beach

Dragline

The Lock

SUSAN GATES

BEWARE the KILLER COAT

Illustrations by Josip Lizatović

WALKER BOOKS
AND SUBSIDIARIES
LONDON • BOSTON • SYDNEY

For Laura, Alex, Christopher and Robert
S.G.

First published 1994 by
Walker Books Ltd, 87 Vauxhall Walk
London SE11 5HJ

This edition published 1995

2 4 6 8 10 9 7 5 3 1

Text © 1994 Susan Gates
Illustrations © 1994 Josip Lizatović

The right of Susan Gates to be identified as author of
this work has been asserted by her in accordance with the
Copyright, Designs and Patents Act 1988.

Printed in England

British Library Cataloguing in Publication Data
A catalogue record for this book
is available from the British Library.

ISBN 0-7445-3666-9

CONTENTS

I knew at once that the coat didn't like me. It scowled at me from a rail in the second-hand shop.

"But I want a new coat!" I told
my mum. "Not a second-hand coat!"
"This is a lovely coat," she said.

I scowled at the coat. The coat
scowled back at me with its rows of
little metal teeth.

It was a big, red, shiny coat, all puffed up like a poison toad. The flaps on the front were wicked green eyes glinting at me. The zips were iron teeth snarling at me. Yes, I hated that coat as soon as I saw it.

"Aren't you lucky to find a coat like this," said Mum. "I can't think why nobody else has bought it!"

But I knew why. It was waiting. Waiting especially for me. And I didn't feel lucky at all!

Try it on, Andrew.

"I'm taking it off. I'm taking it off now, Mum!"

But it wouldn't come off. The coat wouldn't let me go!

Mum tugged and tugged. But the coat held on. It swallowed my head! I was trapped in the dark. The coat clung round my face like an octopus.

I yelled in panic. But the coat crammed my mouth with red shiny stuff so nobody could hear.

Then *pop!* I suddenly saw daylight.
Free at last! Mum had saved me.

"Andrew, you do say the weirdest things! You're letting your imagination run away with you again!"

And she made me carry the coat all the way home.

CHAPTER TWO

After that, the coat behaved itself for
a bit. Then it started eating the notes
I brought home from school. Very
important notes. It did it just to get
me into trouble!

"Andrew!" said my mum. "Why didn't you bring home that note about Parents' Evening?"

"But I put it into my coat pocket. Right after the teacher gave it to me."

I put my hand cautiously through the metal teeth and into the black hole beyond. My hand went down and down, right up to my elbow! There were black tunnels inside the coat, tunnels from every pocket. There was a maze of dark tunnels inside that coat! Quickly I snatched my hand back.

And then my new gloves
disappeared. I didn't lose them.
I put them in my pocket. I know I
did. But the coat ate them. They are
probably still in there, in the coat,
chewed up inside its huge stomach.

And the coat carried on getting bigger and bigger. It swelled up, bulging like a muscle man – getting stronger and fiercer, so that it could get me when nobody was looking.

It's eaten my new gloves. I didn't lose them. Honest!

Sometimes, Andrew, I wonder what's going on inside that head of yours.

They've probably fallen into the lining. Put your hand in and see.

No fear! I wasn't going to put my hand in there, through those metal teeth and deep, deep down inside the coat. What if it grabbed me and chewed my fingers? What if it gnawed them down to the bone? What if, when it had finished, it gave a great belch and let my hand go, and all that was left was a skeleton claw, waggling on the end of my arm?

In the middle of the
night something
woke me up.
What was that
noise? My toes
curled up in
fright. Then I
saw the Killer
Coat hanging on
my bedroom
door. It glowed red
in the darkness. It
was humpy, like a
humped-back troll. It was red and
bulgy, like an Alien Thing from
outer space. I saw a mean, green
eye. It stretched out a long red arm.

Then, *flop!* it leapt down from the peg and a bright red tongue, long as a chameleon's, uncurled. It slithered across the floor!

It was Mum. She switched on the
light. And the Killer Coat just lay
there, good as gold, pretending that
it wasn't creeping up on me.

She picked up the coat. The red
tongue was dangling down its back.
And the coat was grinning at me
with its little silver teeth as if to say,
"Next time, Andrew. Next time.
When we're quite alone."

"And look at this!" said Mum. "Your coat's an even better winter coat than I thought! It's got a nice red hood that you can zip away."

And she rolled up the red tongue and put it behind the shiny teeth.

Then she hung it back, behind my bedroom door.

CHAPTER THREE

The next morning, the coat did its most evil thing yet. It ate my pet rat.

When I had friendly coats, Ratty went everywhere in my pockets.

But I didn't dare put him inside the Killer Coat.

That morning, though, he looked
so miserable locked inside his cage.

At first the coat behaved itself. We
went along the road to school with
Ratty peeping out of my pocket
watching the world go by – just as
he'd done in my old, friendly coat.

When I got into the playground, I reached into my pocket to show Ratty to my friends. But he wasn't there.

I could feel him, running about inside my coat. My friends could see him, trapped beneath the shiny red material.

My coat was moving, wobbling
like a giant strawberry jelly. There
were bulges plopping out all over it!
It was Ratty, in a panic, lost inside
those deep dark tunnels and trying
to get out.

But I knew he would never get
out. The Killer Coat would eat him.

But I knew that Ratty hadn't run away. I knew that he was somewhere deep inside the coat with my new gloves and those very important notes from school – the ones Mum said that I'd lost. Ratty had been gobbled up, like all those other things.

After it had eaten Ratty, the coat grew very big indeed. It swelled up, as if it were proud of itself. It puffed up like a shiny red zeppelin. Its teeth grinned like sharks' teeth. And its mean, green eyes glowed like traffic lights. It was stronger and fiercer than ever. And I knew that it wouldn't be long now. It was only waiting – waiting until we were quite alone.

CHAPTER FOUR

That night I had a dream about the
Killer Coat. I dreamed I tamed it like
a lion-tamer. It growled and roared
and showed its teeth.

But I cracked my lion-tamer's whip and made it afraid of me. It whimpered with fear! I cracked my whip and made it do tricks. I made it jump through burning hoops.

And all the people at the circus cheered and cheered.

But it wasn't true – it was only a
dream. Because when I woke up
next morning the coat was hanging
on the peg behind my bedroom
door. And it wasn't tame at all. It
had grown even bigger, even fiercer
during the night. It seemed to fill
the room.

I looked round my bedroom floor. Why was it so tidy? Where were all my piles of books, my heaps of Lego? The coat had eaten them, so that it would grow stronger and stronger and get me when nobody was there.

You've eaten my computer games! Give them back!

I was really angry. I jumped on
the coat and dragged it off the peg.
We had a terrific fight. I punched and
kicked, but the coat was winning!

It pulled my hair with its metal
teeth.

We rolled over and over, all
round the room. It wrapped me up
in its long slithery arms so I looked
like an Egyptian mummy.

I thumped it, but it wouldn't let me go. It was squeezing me, tighter and tighter!

The bedroom door opened.

"Andrew! What on earth are you doing? Leave that coat alone!"

Phew! Saved again. Just in time.

"I tidied this room up last night," my mum was shouting, "while you were asleep. Now look at the mess in here!"

"It wasn't me," I tried to say. "It was the coat. The coat started it!"

But Mum wasn't listening.

Just look at the state of your coat now!

The coat was lying there, behaving itself, pretending to be good. It let my mother pick it up. It even smiled at her.

My mum carried the coat downstairs and it lay quite still in her arms, like a baby fast asleep.

She said, "This coat's dirty now. I'll have to put it in the washing machine. And when it's clean again, I want you to look after it. Then it'll last the whole winter!"

By then the coat would have got me, for certain. My mum would come to wake me up for school one morning and she'd push my door. But it wouldn't

open. For behind it would be the Great Man-eating Killer Coat, swelling up, filling the whole room, like a big, red, roaring monster! There would be no sign of me. Then the coat would gobble up my mum and grow and grow and burst right through the roof of our house!

It would chase after people, scooping them up with its big red tongue the size of a football field. And when it had eaten all the people on our street, it would move to another street. Then to another town. It would stomp across the countryside and its roars would shake the sky!

It would swim the oceans,
munching whales, nibbling sharks
for snacks.

Nothing could stop it. It would
swell and swell until it filled the
planet, filled the universe...

Andrew! Are
you daydreaming again?
Come and practise
your recorder!

CHAPTER FIVE

Good as gold, the Killer Coat let
Mum put it into the washing
machine. The water rushed into the
machine and the Killer Coat began
to squirm and thrash about.

For a moment I was really scared. I almost ran after my mum shouting, "Wait for me!"

I thought, What if it smashes through the glass to get at me! What if it drags me into the machine and I get washed and rinsed and spun dry! What if…

But then the bubbles frothed and I couldn't see the coat any more. A mean green eye whipped past behind the glass.

Metal teeth scowled at me and vanished in the foam. The Killer Coat spun faster, faster. Now I couldn't see its eyes or teeth at all. It was just a red blur.

And then a strange thing
happened. The white foamy
bubbles began turning red.

What's going on? I thought,
alarmed.

The red whirlpool in the machine
swirled and swirled and swirled
around ... then it rushed away!

I waited. Nothing happened. I crawled to the machine, pressed my nose against the glass and peered inside.

For the Killer Coat wasn't red any more. It was pink. Pale pink! Its eyes were not a fierce and glowing green, but pink as well, like the eyes of white rabbits. And the coat was small now. Not swollen up with shiny red muscles, but shrivelled, like a pink balloon gone pop.

My mum came back into the kitchen.

I tried to look serious. But I was smiling like mad behind my hand. For when my mum pulled out the Killer Coat, all pink and wrinkly, it didn't look dangerous at all. And the best thing was, it wouldn't fit me any more!

I really thought that she was
going to do it. But, at the very last
moment, as she was opening the
back door, something made her
change her mind.

I don't think I will throw it away. Someone might want it. I'll give it to a jumble sale.

I thought I saw the Killer Coat grin at me with its wicked little teeth.

So watch out, if you're going to a jumble sale. Watch out for the Killer Coat. It doesn't look dangerous.

It's pink now, with two pink flaps on the front. But don't be taken in by its disguise. It's still the same old Killer Coat. Don't be fooled if it just lies there, looking good as gold. It's just pretending. It looks small now. But it'll soon start growing. School notes (very important ones) are its favourite snack, and new gloves and pet rats. And *you*, if you're not very, very careful.

Beware the Killer Coat!

MORE WALKER SPRINTERS
For You to Enjoy

☐ 0-7445-3196-9 *Captain Cranko and the Crybaby*
by Jean Ure / Mick Brownfield £2.99

☐ 0-7445-3664-2 *Gemma and the Beetle People*
by Enid Richemont /
Tony Kenyon £2.99

☐ 0-7445-3665-0 *The Biggest Birthday
Card in the World*
by Alison Morgan / Carolyn Dinan £2.99

☐ 0-7445-3183-7 *The Baked Bean Kids*
by Ann Pilling / Derek Matthews £2.99

☐ 0-7445-3173-X *Jolly Roger*
by Colin McNaughton £2.99

☐ 0-7445-3093-8 *The Haunting of Pip Parker*
by Anne Fine /
Emma Chichester Clark £2.99

☐ 0-7445-3188-8 *Beware Olga!*
by Gillian Cross / Arthur Robins £2.99

**Walker Paperbacks are available from most booksellers,
or by post from B.B.C.S., P.O. Box 941, Hull, North Humberside HU1 3YQ**

24 hour telephone credit card line 01482 224626

To order, send: Title, author, ISBN number and price for each book ordered, your full
name and address, cheque or postal order payable to BBCS for the total amount and allow
the following for postage and packing: UK and BFPO: £1.00 for the first book, and 50p
for each additional book to a maximum of £3.50. Overseas and Eire: £2.00 for the first
book, £1.00 for the second book and 50p for each additional book.

Prices and availability are subject to change without notice.

Name _____

Address _____

_____